This book belongs to:

• •

• •

• •

Treasure Beach

Yasmine Case
ISBN: 9798393667085

Dad

Jaxon

Mum

Meet the characters!

Barnie

Gerrard

Cody

This is Jaxon, he loves adventures!

He likes exploring the great outdoors, dressing up as pirates and searching for treasure with his dog Barnie.

Jaxon spends lots of time playing in his garden.

But when the weather turns bad, it's time to play indoors.

The stormy winds blew. Jaxon stared out of his bedroom window, the rain was falling hard and fast.

"oh, no!" Jaxon cried. "If the storm doesn't stop soon, we won't be able to visit Treasure Beach tomorrow!"

Jaxon's Mum laughed and said "It will be okay, sometimes the best time to go to the beach is just after a storm.
If we dress for the weather we will be able to enjoy the beach whether rain, or shine.
The best sea treasure can be found after a storm."

Jaxon's Mum tucked him in to bed and then found the perfect bedtime story.

The book was called Fossil Treasure!

Jaxon snuggled in to his bed and cuddled up to Barnie as his mum began to read.

As Jaxon started to fall
asleep, he whispered
"Tomorrow is going
to be one big adventure."

After a good night's sleep, Jaxon woke up happy and refreshed. The skies are beginning to clear and everyone in the house is busy getting ready. Today's the day he goes to treasure beach.

Jaxon starts to look through his things and tries to decide what he should take for his adventure, but he's a bit unsure as to what to pack.

Can you help Jaxon find what he needs to take with him to the beach?

Mum is making the most delicious
surprise picnic.

Dad is packing the car.

Everyone is ready and off they go.
The excitement bubbled up inside
Jaxon as they drove closer and closer
to the beach.

when they arrive Dad goes over
the beach pirate rules. Jaxon knows
the rules very well but it's always
good to be reminded.

Jaxon was very good at following the pirate rules. He begun exploring and searching for treasure with Barnie's help.

Barnie began to dig a big hole, they were bound to find something interesting. There is so much to see and so much to find.

As Jaxon looked closely between
the stones, the sun began to shine.
An object reflected the suns light and
caught Jaxon's eye.
But 'what did he find?'

Jaxon shouted his Mum and Dad
to come and have a look,
Barnie gave it a sniff.
The object was very dirty and old,
but as he rubbed it between his
fingers he could see gold.
It was real pirate treasure!

Jaxon was filled with excitement and rushed to find his bucket to wash the treasure.

He rubbed it and scrubbed it until it sparkled. It was the most amazing old gold ring.

Jaxon spent the rest of the day searching for more treasure with a smile across his face.

He found sea glass and sea crystals, which were all sorts of sizes, perfectly smooth and frosty looking.

Jaxon even used his magnifying glass
to find the most terrific fossils.

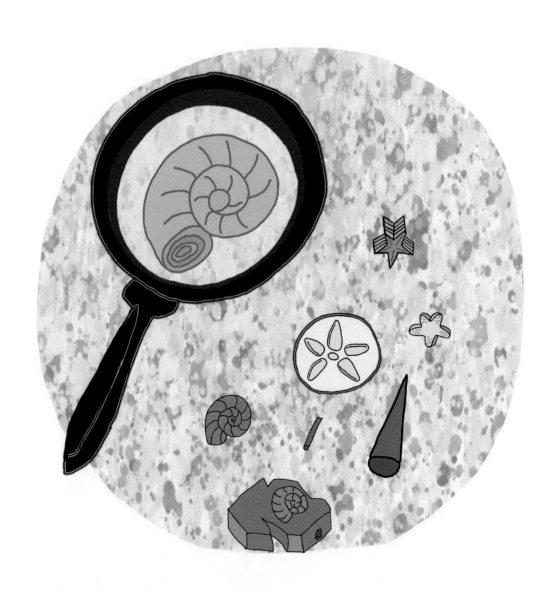

After finding so many treasures
it was time for a rest,
and some much needed food.

Mum asked "what are we going to do with the sea treasure?"
Jaxon commented
"Make sea pictures, of course! And now I have a magnificent real pirate ring, Barnie and I can be pirates at home."

As they were leaving the beach something caught Jaxon's eye.

Can you guess what he found?

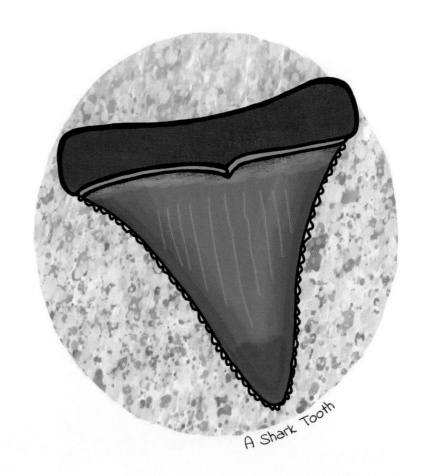

A Shark Tooth

what a brilliant day!

Thank you for reading and I hope you enjoyed the story. Please support my book by leaving a review.
You may also like

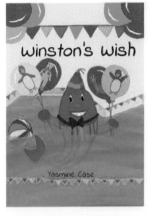

Follow the author here on Facebook

Children's Books by Yasmine

Printed in Great Britain
by Amazon

30002407R00023